CHICAGO PUBLIC LIBRARY
CLEARING
6423 W.
CHICAGO,
312-747-

NOV

D0284740

DISCARD

To:

From:

Eloise's Christmas Trinkles

KAY THOMPSON'S

ELOISE's
Christmas Trinkles

CHICAGO PUBLIC LIBRARY
CLEARING BRANCH
6423 W. 63RD PL.
CHICAGO, IL 60638
312-747-5657

Drawings by HILARY KNIGHT

Simon & Schuster Books for Young Readers

NEW YORK · LONDON · TORONTO · SYDNEY

R0415165673

Once there was this little child
You know her I believe
Here's who she is me ELOISE
And it is Christmas Eve

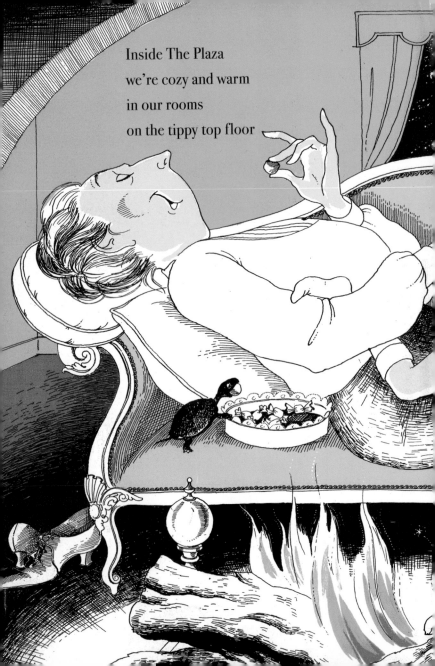

Inside The Plaza
we're cozy and warm
in our rooms
on the tippy top floor

We're Skipperdee who is my turtle
and Weenie who is my dog
Nanny my mostly companion
and ME and the blazing Yuletide log

While Nanny is filling the stockings
I shout out loud and clear
"I must go down
to the lobby
to spread some Christmas cheer"

And Nanny says
"Of course
of course
of course
you must my dear"

Then I jingle out to the elevator

All of the cars are full
to the brim
because of the holiday
God rest ye merry gentlemen
Let nothing you dismay

It is rawther crowded

And you should see the lobby
You absolutely cawn't get near it
There are all these people
roaming around
filled with the Christmas spirit

I usually wear a star or so
in case there is this package
that doesn't know where it's going

Then it's zippity jingle and dash away ping
Hang holly and berries all in the halls
Tie tassels on all the thermostats and
write Merry Christmas on all of the walls

I go to as many holiday parties as I possibly can

I have to do quite a bit
of trimming
for it's Christmas Eve tonight
Trim trinkles and drinkles
and sklinkles of glass
Trim everything in sight

I always hang a star on top
with angels in between

Here's how many lights we have
thirty-seven and sixteen

I am giving the bellboys earmuffs
the waiters baseball socks
Thomas is getting a vest with a bib
Room Service a music box

And for my friend Vincent the barber
this rawther unusual brush
with rawther unusual bristles
that got caught in the Christmas rush

But wrap it oh wrap it oh holly oh Christmas
in tinsel and ribbon and paste
Then stick with a sticker a seal and a card
TO THE BARBERSHOP POSTHASTE

I'm giving Mr. Harris in catering
a pair of woollen gloves
and a piece of fruitcake from Japan
which he absolutely loves

I got a present for Nanny for Nanny for Nanny
but I don't tell her
It's a little silver thimble full of
frankincense and myrrh

For Weenie a roast-beef bone deluxe
For Skipperdee raisin milk
I'm giving the valet a beehive of course
made of safety pins and silk

And when my gifts are delivered and wrapped
and put under the tree tree tree
I have to trim this children's one
for Weenie and Skipperdee

I'm rawther fond of caroling

Fa la on every floor

Fa la la la to catering

Fa la from door to door

We sang Noel for 506

Silent Night for 507

We didn't sing for 509
at the request of 511

My mother called
long distance
from the Mediterranean
I believe
We talked for an hour and
charged it
like we did last Christmas Eve

She was sunburned on her legs
and sent me this absolutely
sweet cartwheel hat
with these earpuffs on it

Then Nanny stretched and yawned out loud
and cheerily inquired

"What *are* we doing
up up up
when we're so tired tired tired?"

"Let's jingle to bed
    Now there's a girl
    Let's have no tears of sorrow
    Let's close our eyes
    and sleep sleep sleep
    so we can carry on tomorrow"

I always hang a two-legged Christmas stocking just in case

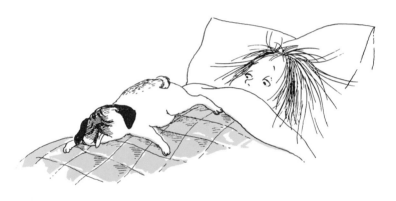

Some of us were rawther tired

Then some of us sort of closed some of our eyes
to have us this Christmas dream

of some steaming hot plum pudding
with extra cream cream cream

of reindeers with sunglasses on
ice-skating on the stars
with mittens on their antlers
and mufflers made in Mars

And Santa chuckled and said
"Dash on to The Plaza my lovely boys
We'll have Christmas punch with Nanny
and give Eloise her toys"

I thought he looked terribly well

And when we awakened
he'd come and gone
and in all of this midnight and dark
we could see these reindeers zimbering
through the trees in Central Park

We could even see this taillight
on Santa Claus' sleigh

Then oh oh oh absolutely oh oh
Oh trinkles and sklinkles of glee
Oh look oh look oh *will* you look
at the presents under the tree

And in all of this
everly Christmas excitement
we could hardly wait to see

What Nanny gave Weenie
What Weenie gave Emily
What Nanny gave Emily
What Weenie gave Nanny
What Emily gave Nanny
What Emily gave Weenie
What Skipperdee gave Weenie and Emily and Nanny
What Nanny and Emily and Weenie gave Skipperdee
And of course what they all

gave me

And everyone shouted and yelled oh oh oh
and unwrapped the Christmas surprise
And some us couldn't believe what
we saw
with some of our Christmas eyes

And there it was
and it sparkled at me
A diamond necklace of trinkles and glue
"Oh trinkles" I said
"Nanny dear I love you
I absolutely do"

Here is who my absolutely best friend
in this whole wide world is
Nanny

Then it's up and it's oh
to the telephone go
"Hello there Room Service dear
Send Christmas breakfast
on Christmas trays
to these four Christmas children
up here

"And if you'd like
to nibble on something
like some Christmas
cinnamon trees
simply tell the chef
to bake some at once
and charge it to me
ELOISE"

They're absolutely delicious

"It's absolutely Christmas
so come to the top floor please
come all of my friends wherever you are
For a trinkle with
ME
ELOISE"

Jingle
here
jingle
there
jingle
Christmas
everywhere

jingle

jingle

jingle

Ooooooooooooooooooooooo!

I absolutely love Christmas

SIMON & SCHUSTER BOOKS FOR YOUNG READERS
An imprint of Simon & Schuster Children's Publishing Division
1230 Avenue of the Americas, New York, New York 10020
Copyright © 2007 by the Estate of Kay Thompson
Adapted from *Eloise at Christmastime* copyright © 1958 by Kay Thompson,
copyright renewed © 1986 by Kay Thompson

All rights reserved, including the right of reproduction in whole or in part in any form.
SIMON & SCHUSTER BOOKS FOR YOUNG READERS is a trademark of Simon & Schuster, Inc.
"Eloise" and related marks are trademarks of the Estate of Kay Thompson.

Book design by Marc Cheshire
The text for this book is set in ITC Bodoni Seventy-Two.
Manufactured in the United States of America
2 4 6 8 10 9 7 5 3 1
Library of Congress Cataloging-in-Publication Data
Kay Thompson's Eloise's Christmas trinkles / drawings by Hilary Knight.
— 1st ed. • p. cm.
Summary: Six-year-old Eloise, determined to spread Christmas cheer throughout the Plaza Hotel, "decorates"
the halls, distributes unusual gifts to the staff, and goes door-to-door singing carols for the surprised guests.
ISBN-13: 978-0-689-87425-3 • ISBN-10: 0-689-87425-1
[1. Christmas–Fiction. 2. Plaza Hotel (New York, N.Y.)–Fiction. 3. Hotels, motels, etc.–Fiction.
4. Humorous stories. 5. Stories in rhyme.] I. Knight, Hilary, ill. II. Thompson, Kay, 1909-1998.
III. Title: Eloise's Christmas trinkles.
PZ8.3.K2253 2007 • [E]–dc22 • 2007003978

first
edition